Acknowledgement

I want to dedicate this book to my wife

Charita and my three kids Desmond, Maiya

and Amari. They say the first book is the

hardest and I must agree. I might have waited

too late to start trying to put my thoughts on

paper. This book series is a part of my process

of growing and reinventing myself. This book

is loosely based on some of my interactions as

a bail bondsman. The names and the stories

have been changed. Any similarities should be

considered a coincidence in other words some

of the characters are fictional. I want to give

special thanks to Deva, Carter, June and Latina

for their contributions. As you read this book,

you will notice that it is suitable for all ages

and that it is not a very long book. The plan is

to create entertaining short stories that will not take a lot of time to read. I hope you enjoy the first book: BAIL LIFE VOLUME 1

Going back to when I was young, I learned to always try to think ahead. It's just a trait that I picked up from my Mom. She was a tough woman, nick-named "Mitch". I never knew how she got that name, but you could always tell, by the way people responded to her when she showed up, she was well respected. She could give a look that could kill when she was upset. My mom didn't take any mess. My dad showed her the "utmost" respect, especially when she would give orders around the house.

My Dad, on the other hand, was laid back. Nothing ever bothered him. He had a very sneaky way of getting his point across, with a cunning sense of humor and a sly smile when he would slip a joke past you. I guess I got my personality from both. From mom, I got my toughness and I got my patience to weigh out decisions from my father. I grew up in a neighborhood full, of good people and not so good people. Just like most kids, it was hard to tell which was which, until they stole your bike or threw rocks at you. Just by looking at a person you couldn't tell the difference.

I am also an athlete, playing every sport, but I fell in love with basketball. Every day after school I was on the court and sometimes I played in my backyard or at a gym. When I was in middle school, I kind of got a reputation for being tricky on the court. That's how I got the name DOC, mainly after the great Doctor J a.k.a. Julius Erving, my idol. He was an assassin on the court and worshipped by most basketball players in the early 70's. It was on the basketball court that I met a guy that changed my life. He laid the foundation for my career in Bail bonding and Bounty Hunting.

His name was Ralph Sell, Ralph had several businesses and he did Bail Bonding on the side. He used to bail out people that worked for him if they got arrested over the weekends. When he got them out of jail he could take the money out of their checks. I started working with Ralph in the bail bond business, when I was twenty-nine years old. What we do as a bail bondsman is put up money to get people out of jail. If they show up for court, everything's fine. If they skip on the bond, we have to go find them and put them back in jail. Overall, it is a gamble. We are betting we can find them if they skip court. If we do, we can keep our money. The court gives us five months time to find them or the money's gone. Now, Ralph didn't really want to be involved with the business too much other than getting the money. This is why we didn't stay in business together too long.

One day, we had a bail skip over in a Hispanic neighborhood called Travelers Rest. It was a trailer park on the East side of Burlington, North Carolina. The East side of town was more impoverished than the West, by design. We had one of our acquaintances to set him up and get him drunk. I called Ralph to come with me to pick him up, but he started making excuses. His excuses were like a guy trying to get off work, right after payday. So, I went over and picked the bail skip up by myself. Fortunately, when I caught up with the skip, he was laying on the couch drunk. Before he had realized it, I was putting him in handcuffs.

A little while later, Me and Ralph finally went separate ways. I got a bond call and Ralph followed me to jail and started writing bond, but he didn't want to give me my split of the commission. The deal was to split the commissions fifty-fifty. That was the last day of me and Ralph.

Back then, It took five thousand dollars to become a bail bondsman. I talked to the one person that I knew had that kind of money, good old Mom. She fronted me the money and I told her I would pay her back in six months. Six months later, I paid her back, with interest.

The Bonding part came pretty easy for me, since in Burlington, there weren't any black owned bail bond businesses and most of the guys in the area knew me from playing basketball. Part of my thinking was that, "who else were the guys going to call that they could trust".

I grew up in the hood. I knew the rules of hustling, "keep your mouth shut", "keep your eyes open" and "know a lot more than you say". Bail Bonding also has another side to it. We have to work with law enforcement. Working first hand with the police, you see a lot of things when you are around the jail, but the same rules apply for the Police as they do for the hood. If you hear about a big bust coming, you keep your mouth shut and wait for the phone calls. I never broke those rules and business has been great.

I've only got one runner, Big Deva. Basically, a runner does the same thing as I do as a bondsman, except they don't have to pay if the bond goes bad. I met big Deva at Elon University sitting in a criminal justice class. I was working with the instructor. Deva was six foot six, three hundred forty pounds and very confident. The professor introduced us after class and I asked him if he could get up and down the court at his size. He always told me not to let the size fool me, he was quicker than he looked. Deva was from Caswell County way down in the country. He got to Elon College on a basketball scholarship. He was an aggressive player and some people would consider "aggressive" an understatement by the way he played ball. Deva and I have worked together for a long time now and are more like brothers.

This first case was difficult because we had to track a client to Virginia. Bail bonding has gotten more regulated and more strict over time, because of mistakes. First, a bondsman in Texas broke into the wrong house and another bondsman went to Virginia and tried to arrest the sheriff of the town. He mistook the sheriff for his cousin. In all honesty, they did look a lot alike. That Sheriff didn't have such a great sense of humor. When they finished that case, NC bail bondsmen were banned from working in the State of Virginia and that particular bondsman was put in prison.

It starts when I get a call from Putt, he is one of my street informant's. I am at a sporting goods store looking at some new golf irons when I hear my phone ring.

Locked Up they want let me out,
no they want let me out.
Maybe a visit they want let me out
 send me some magazines they want let me out
send me some money orders

That's my ring and ring back tone, so people can feel Akon's pain, when thinking about getting a loved one out of jail. If they're not going to get the person out of jail, the least they could do is visit, send some money, or some magazines.

Putt: Hey Doc what up?

Me: What's up Putt?

Putt: Hey man, your boy Roosevelt went over to Newport Virginia.

Me: When did he go over there?

Putt: He went over there about a month ago, I think he's staying with an uncle or something.

Me: I got five thousand on him this time, and now he decides to go to the beach. I appreciate the love. I will call you if something comes up later.

Putt: Alright, I appreciate you getting me out last week. I didn't know what I was going to do.

Locked Up they want let me out,
No... they want let me out.
Maybe a visit, they want let me out
Send me some magazines, they won't let me out
Send me some money orders

The phone rings constantly during the day. I count over 100 calls. I probably only do eight bonds, the rest are people in the jail, wanting to make a deal of some sorts on their bond or it is someone wanting a phone call to someone that didn't really want to hear from them. Some calls were from my informants with info on skips on the run. Occasionally, a call from the family will come in.

Locked Up they want let me out,
No… they want let me out.
Maybe a visit, they want let me out
Send me some magazines, they won't let me out
Send me some money orders

Charita: Can you bring home some lottery tickets one and two dollar ones, when you come in?

Me: O yeah, I maybe a little late.

Charita: that's OK.

I came out great, when it came to the wife picking department. My wife is beautiful with a great sense of humor. I stay out of the way when she is on a project and with three kids she's busy. My oldest children have moved out. Desmond, my son is in the Air Force; Maiya, my creative artist is an actress and the youngest is Amari. She is thirteen and wants to be a doctor.

In jail,
In jail without no bail,
In jail,
We're in jail, because we failed
(Deva's ring back tone is an old Fat Boys song)

Me: Hey Deva, I got some info own Roosevelt he's over there in Virginia, at an Uncle's house.
Deva: Where at.
Me: New Port, kind of near Virginia Beach.

Deva: you got an address?

Me: Not yet, I'm going to call Latina to do a background check and find out where his relatives live. I should have something later on today.

Deva: Just let me know, I'm going to go work out.

    I called the office and told Latina to check to see who Roosevelt was kin to in New Port, especially his Uncles. Latina was from Puerto Rican descent. She's super smart and quick; I met her when she was going through an abusive divorce with her ex-husband. She was at the jail filing a complaint when a friend of ours introduced us. Her friend knew I was a bail bondsman and thought I could be of help.

Later on that week, she showed up at the office looking for some work and she's been with us every since.

Locked Up, they want let me out,
No.... they want let me out.
Maybe a visit, they want let me out
Send me some magazines, they won't let me out
Send me some money orders

Me: Hello

Ricky: How much would it be to get out of jail if I knock this woman in the head? (hollering in the background)

Me: What do you mean?

Ricky: I'm about to knock this Chick out, she drank up all my liquor while I was sleep. How much would my bond be?

Me: You already know, they don't like you down there and depending on which Magistrate is there you might not get a bond. You, probably, just need to leave. (hollering in the back ground)

Unknown female: Try it! I wish you would. Come on, don't talk about it!

Ricky: Man, I can't stand her sometimes. She's crazy as hell and drunk. You're right though about my record, I can't afford another charge.

Me: Man, you need me to find you another place to stay.

Ricky: I'll call you back. (click)

I also do real estate on the side. This week I am listing a nice three-bedroom two-bath home in Graham. My motto is, "I can put you in a Big House" or "I can get you out of the Big House". I only list a few properties and that's by design. Sometimes, It takes me up to five or six months to find a buyer. The real estate business takes a little more time. We have to negotiate price and have things repaired. With the economy like it is now, you have to be diversified. Owning these two different businesses can really be challenging at times. With one business, people want your help and with the other business, people need your help. It is interesting to see how people act. In Bail bonding, a person is going to find the money and spend it to get your people out of jail. There is no way around it. In the real estate market, people can shop around and take their time.

Locked Up, they want let me out,
No... they want let me out.
Maybe a visit, they want let me out
send me some magazines, they won't let me out
send me some money orders

Me: Hello.

Latina: Hey, his Uncle Henry lives on 111 Starmont Lane in New Port Va. He's owned the house for about six years, he's single, and works at the Recreation Department there, he drives a 2010 Ford Fusion...

Me: Thanks Latina, me and Deva's going to head up that way pretty soon.

Latina: Be careful.

Me: O yeah, just shutdown the office when you leave.

Phone ringing.

Charita: hello?

Me: I'm going to New Port Virginia, in a few, I got a skip over there that needs a ride back to jail.

Charita: When are you coming back.

Me: hopefully tonight.

Charita: Is Deva going with you?

Me: I'm getting ready to call him right now.

Charita: I thought you weren't supposed to go to Virginia and pick up people.

Me: Keep your phone on just in case (I get into trouble), I'll talk to you later.

On our way to New Port, Deva and I go over different plans of how we are going to get in the house and how we are going to make sure he is there before we hit the door. I came up with the *taxi guy trick*. I call a random cab company, which ends up being yellow cab. The driver is an older black man with a hint of gray showing on both sides of his head and a little goatee. The glasses he wears have transition lenses that seemed to have a few years past their prime. I ask him if he was willing to make an extra fifty dollars? He says, "It depends". I ask him to pull in the yard and blow, then go to the door and see if you recognize him. I show him a picture and give him half the money. We wait for about ten minutes. We see the cab driver come around the corner. He says, he was 98% sure it was him and the guy had an attitude about him knocking on the door. Cursed him out saying, "he didn't call no cab".

Deva gives me a confirming nod and a hard expression goes across his face. I would compare it to game face. I pay the taxi driver the other half of the money and thank him for his time. We load up: Taser, check; Glock, check; flashlight, check; cuffs, check. We are ready to ride. It is a three minute drive from where we are staged to get to the house.

It is a white house with a small porch and the windows shade was open a little. The time is about 6:30 pm. There is a church across from the house. We pull into the parking lot and angle the car so that we can see the house. We watch the house and survey the surrounding area. Our standard procedure is for Deva to go to the backdoor and wait for the escape attempt. We start walking up to the house, Deva goes down the right side of the house and I ease up on the porch and look in the window. I see my guy lying on the couch, watching TV. I knock on the door, he looks up agitated and starts walking over to the door. He looks out of the door like a deer in headlights. I say, "Bail Bondsman!" He immediately starts running to the back. I pull the screen door handle so hard it comes off in my hand while I am kicking on the front door. The door flies open on the second kick. I pull my taser and follow him toward the back of the house. I hear Deva yell,

"Doc" and I run straight to the back door. I see him trying to get away from Deva's grasp, so, I fire the taser at him. He and Deva both go to the ground. I hear Deva going, "urrrh", "urrrh" (grunting). I cut the power to the taser and handcuff Roosevelt. Deva gets up and I see the taser cord was under Deva. Evidently by Deva having his hands on Roosevelt, the current went through him and knocked them both down.

Me: You alright Deva?
Deva: Yeah, I'm good.
Roosevelt: Doc, I was coming back to take care of it.
Me: Yeah, you were on your way out the back door to go take care of it. Riiight.

Roosevelt: Man, Can I get my money and some cigarettes.

Me: Where's the money, I don't do no smoking in the car.

Roosevelt: It's in my room, let me leave a note for my Uncle and pull the door to. You didn't have to kick it in.

Getting those cuffs on a.s.a.p. is always a practice of mine. If a person is given time to think they will always make a bad decision. When we get to the car, I switch the lucky cuffs out for the short chains. This way, he can have his hands in the front, since it is going to be a long ride back to Burlington. Then, we hook the leg irons on so he can't jump and run. Three and a half hours later we are at the

Alamance County Jail, doing a "surrender". We don't relax until we're walking out with our "surrender" sheet.

I get home around twelve midnight. There are no lights on except for the one to let me know all is well and I was thought of while I was away. Its like tying a yellow ribbon around an oak tree. I come in, cut the lights off and proceed to the den, where I can decompress. After each pick up, I take time to reflect on how it went and what I could have done differently. I might have held off on shooting him with the taser until Deva was clear, Just a thought.

The next morning I go with the cereal option for breakfast. Amari is moving around, getting ready for school. My wife takes her to school and then comes back home. Her day consists of taking care of her aging Mom and Dad. I grab my bag, when she gets back and give her the "eye". I can tell if I need to stay a little longer by the look she returns my query. Today's look is, "I don't have time for that."

Me: Your Mom doing ok?

Charita: As well as she can, she still has good and bad days.

Me: I'll try to be in early tonight, I need to get caught up on some sleep. (eyebrows raised and tilt of the head)

Charita: I know that look. We'll see... (with a big smile)

The office is about five miles from my house and directly across from the jail, which is very convenient. As soon as I get in, I start doing the paper work on the pickup. We have to notify the court system that Roosevelt is in custody. Serving the court are the District Attorney and the School Board Attorney. Our district attorney really just passes the paper through the system and makes sure the client gets a court date. The School Board Attorney's job is to get as much money as he can for the school system. If I don't find my guy in five months or make any other mistake in doing the bond, he can take me to court and try to get the money I posted or more.

Locked Up, they want let me out,
No... they want let me out.

Maybe a visit, they want let me out

send me some magazines, they won't let me out

send me some money orders

Me: Hello.

Jail call from Ricky: Hey Doc my bond is Two Thousand dollars, how much is that?

Me: It's Three hundred, what happened.

Ricky: I left like you said, but I came back to get some stuff and she would not stop running that mouth,

so, I smacked her.

Me: Is she hurt?

Ricky: Naw, she beat my tail, I'm the one that called the police. They sent 2 women officers, so when I saw they were just looking at her side, I decided to run and they tased me. They arrested her too because of my marks. I need to get her out too; I can't let her stay in jail.

Me: (muffled chuckling) Man that's funny.

Ricky: Man, are you coming to get me or not?

Me: I'll get Deva to come down. Do you have the money?

Ricky: I get paid on Friday. I got a hundred now.

Me: Alright, call you guys a ride home.

Deva's not the fastest at getting to the jail, but he will go every time, especially since he gets paid on commission. He gets a percent of everything he writes. It usually takes about an hour and a half to write the bond and get the person out of jail. While I'm at the office, people stop by just to talk about current events. My main man Carter comes by almost every day just to talk about the sports, mostly golf. Carter is retired from the Gary, Indiana School system and is 78 years old. He is well preserved for his age. He still plays golf two or three times a week and hits the ball further than me somehow. It probably has something to do with those big hands he has. Carter was a MP in the army after his college football days.

Carter: My man, What's going on?

Me: Had to go to Virginia to get a skip.

Carter: You get him?

Me: Yep, no problems.

Carter: Good (with a fist pump) what time are those boys playing golf tomorrow?

Me: Ten, are you playing?

Carter: I might make it out there depends on this old knee when I wake up. You never know what kind of shape that things going to be in when you wake up.

I turn the TV to the golf channel so we can catch up on the Honda classic. I started playing golf seriously about twenty years ago, when I noticed my injuries were starting to pile up from the basketball court. Golf is a game, my parents played when I was young, but I avoided it for years. Now, I'm hooked. I even have a handicap of around an eight. Most of the time we have a group of twelve to sixteen retirees and a few hustlers trying to make a dollar off whoever's not putting their time in practicing.

After visiting with Carter and solving several of the problems of today's politics, I start working on our next skip, Calvin Lang. Calvin is a pretty bad guy that has moved to Hillsborough from DC. He has a bad reputation for robbing and shooting people. The more I look for him, the more people I hear he has shot. A while ago, Calvin was arrested with a regular client of mine, Jerry Jones. He gave a fake name "Terry Harris" to the officer and the jail's computer system was down. I bailed out Calvin because that he was with Jerry and the system didn't identify him as somebody that I could not trust. The bond I posted was two thousand dollars.

He and Jerry were riding in a truck that they had borrowed from a crack head. They were pulled for the tags being out of date. Jerry jumped out of the truck and ran. Calvin set back, relaxed and waited. The officer caught up to Jerry and he tried to pull a gun on the officer. Somehow, the officer didn't shoot him. Jerry laid his gun down and Lang was arrested with him. Jerry's mom came down, as usual, to bail out her baby. Most of the time, I give the guys a good sermon on how lucky they are not to be dead right now, but Jerry had a different look about him this time. Usually, he was joking around, this time he had a look as though he could see right through me. Jerry's bond was twenty thousand and his mom came down with half the money. So, I set him up on payments. Calvin paid three hundred dollars for his two thousand dollar bond.

About three weeks later, I get a call from Calvin

Calvin: Hey Doc, I know you are Jerry's people and all so, I'm going to let you know I can't go to court, I gave you the wrong name. I got warrants and I can't show up for court.

Me: O yeah?

Calvin: Don't worry, I'm going to send you, your two thousand dollars before court.

Me: Send it to my office in Graham 137 W. Elm St.

Calvin: Got it, sorry about that, Man.

Calvin's court date came and went without a word. I found out his real name was Calvin Lang from a visit by the State Bureau of Investigations. When the jail ran his fingerprints, they got a hit once the system came back up. He had already made bail, and I was the one that had done the bond. That makes me responsible for him. The S.B.I. paid me a visit, to get any information that I might have had on him. While at the office, they tell me they are investigating Calvin for a double murder and robbery case that I was familiar with in Caswell County. I actually had worked with the guy that got killed when I was an employee with the City. The Sheriffs found him and his wife tied up at the kitchen table, shot and their trailer burned. Calvin Lang is their person of interest.

The first thing I like to do when I am hunting a person is to get all the information I can about him or her. Every bondsman has people that live and survive in the streets with a tendency to go to jail every now and then. Keeping them out of jail helps when you need a favor.

Phone ringing.

Poochie: Hey baby, how you doing?

Me: I'm good, how about you?

Poochie: You know I'm good. Hey, I just got a new job over at Pizzeria. I'm cooking pizzas.

Me: Really, that's great, how long you been there?

Poochie: About a two weeks now, they love me there, I'm even starting to gain a little weight.

Me: I know they do, you work hard when you work. Hey, what do you know about a guy named Calvin Lang.

Poochie: You mean C Murk from Hillsborough, He's bad news, he goes around robbing drug dealers and shooting them most of the time. He's the one that shot Roberto that time.

Me: Where does he hang at?

Poochie: He lives in Hillsborough, I think you need to give that guy a pass or let someone else get him. He's crazy. I'll let you know, if I hear something though. Say a prayer for me. You know, I'm a work in progress.

Me: (Chuckle) we all are, I will.

Most of my clients have an appreciation for my ability to keep a moral standard, even around the underworld. You have to keep your distance. I also understand how people end up where they are in life. Some people don't have a chance. They are born or raised in a bad place. If you are raised thinking you are supposed to struggle and you see everyone around you struggling, most likely you will stay in that pattern. How can you do better than your parents? When they are supposed to be the people to guide you. Sometimes, it's too late when you figure out mom was a crack head.

With that info in hand, I make a call to Latina to get Calvin's family and friends info. *Phone ringing.*

Latina: Hey Boss...

Me: Funny, can you get me Calvin Lang's girlfriend, baby moma, family or any locations he's been arrested in?

Latina: Sure, no problem, O yeah, someone called from the Positive Attitude Youth Center called they wanted to know if you were going to keep your ad in their book for this year

Me: How much is it?

Latina: The same as last year.

Me: Ok, I'll get a check over there this week.

Latina: I'll give you a call when I come up with something.

Me: Thanks, I'm heading to Hillsborough to talk with the Orange County Sheriff office.

Just for the record, I love the Sheriff of Alamance County, he has to be one of the toughest in the country. You can tell when you cross the line into Orange County, things change drastically. In all fairness to Orange County's Sheriff Department, they have the Chapel Hill side and the Hillsborough side. The Chapel Hill side gets most of the attention and resources, since they have the University of Chapel Hill there. It's about a twenty-minute drive to Hillsborough and way past my lunchtime. I stop by Bo Jangles for a two-piece dark meat with dirty rice and a Cheerwine soda. Only people from the South can relate to this indulgence.

Locked Up, they want let me out,
No... they want let me out.
Maybe a visit, they want let me out
Send me some magazines, they won't let me out
Send me some money orders

Me: What's up, Deva?

Deva: We had a couple of forfeitures come in today, one of them was ten thousand.

Me: Who is it?

Deva: Alex Chandler, he had a bond for Possession of cocaine with intent to sell.

Me: Pull the file and see what you can find out about him. Who was the other one?

Deva: Bobby Tucker, I'll give him a call, an see what's up. I can't believe he keeps missing court.

Me: Thanks Deva, I'll talk to you later, I'm pulling up to the Orange County Sheriffs office.

The sheriff office in Hillsborough is a pretty small place with about six cars on the outside and a couple of officers inside. Lieutenant Scott was my point of contact. Scott is a tall man, with a bald head and a bad attitude. He didn't want to be bothered today, as usual.

Me: I'm Michael Doc Reaves, I'm a bail bondsman from Alamance County, I was wondering if you guys have heard anything about a guy named Calvin Lang.

Scott: O yeah, I know him well. His girlfriend works down at Play Hard Worx, the sex shop, her name is Christie Atwater. I tell you one thing, we wouldn't go after him without the S.W.A.T. team. He already said he wasn't going back to jail. Have you heard anything?

Me: O yeah, everything I've heard is that he's around here somewhere.

Scott: I've heard is, he's in Alamance County robbing folk.

Me: Do you know where his girlfriend lives?

Scott: Yeah, she lives in the Vine apartments off Hwy 70.

Me: Ok, I appreciate your help, I'll let you know when I get him.

It's something to be said for not burning bridges in this business, even though I can sense the unwillingness to help out. You never know what could happen down the road. Since I am already over in Hillsborough, I might as well pay Christie a little visit; no harm in talking. I get motivated once I decide to close something out.

The Vine apartments aren't in too bad of shape. You would think people living here would be doing alright for themselves. I guess the police have had a few calls to her apartment. They are able to give me the address from memory.

(knock, knock, knock)

Christie: hello

Me: Hey, how's it going? Is Calvin home?

Christie: No, Calvin doesn't live here. I've already told the sheriffs and Police that. Who are you anyway, and who told you where I live?

Me: I'm Doc, I bailed Calvin out in Alamance, about two months ago. Calvin didn't go to court.

Christie: Well that don't have nothing to do with me, we broke up a long time ago.

     I study her while we are talking. I can tell she is about a twenty-five year old with a little edge. I assume she came from a good family. She is slim with very distinct curves, dark brown skin tone and long black straight hair.

The house is clean compared to a lot of the houses I go in. She has a picture of Calvin on a table across from where I am standing and a son who looked to be around four or five playing with a remote controlled truck.

Me: You know, I get lied to everyday while I'm doing this and I understand it. No one wants to see someone they love go to jail. Here's my card, if something changes give me a call. I'm going to get him either way.

Christie: Well, you do what you got to do.

Me: Do you have Calvin's phone number so I can give him a call?

Christie: I told you, we don't talk. I think you need to leave.

Me: No problem, I'll be seeing you.

Christie: Right... (with attitude)

On my way back to Burlington, I am thinking about all the information I acquired from being in Hillsborough. Its 5:30.

Locked Up they want let me out,
No they want let me out.
Maybe a visit they want let me out
Send me some magazines they won't let me out
Send me some money orders

Me: Reaves

Calvin: Hey man, I don't like you going over to my girls place sweating her.

Me: Who is this? (I know its Calvin)

Calvin: You know who it is. I told you I was going to give you your money. I don't like you going by my girls house, she don't have nothing to do with this.

Me: Hey Calvin, we just need to see each other, where you at?

Calvin: I don't live around there. I'm in Durham.

Me: Where can we meet up?

Calvin: I'll get in touch with you when I get the money.

Me: Riiiight. (phone goes dead).

I drive a 2013 Toyota Avalon, it has the touch screen and navigation system and ports for everything. It also doubles as my family car. I have a car to drive when I want to creep around, but you can only drive it a nighttime. You only have to be seen out in it one time, before the streets know your car. Most Detective cars are easy to spot. I choose a Toyota because there's so many out there and the higher end cars draw extra attention when you go to the projects.

Locked Up they want let me out,
No they want let me out.
Maybe a visit they want let me out
Send me some magazines they won't let me out
Send me some money orders

Me: hello

Telemarketer: You have just qualified for free points toward travel to any destination...

Me: I'm not interested. (click)

I don't like getting telemarketing calls, but I can't keep them off the business line. When I get to the office, Latina was gone and had left notes on Calvin and Alex. I decide to call it an early day and go by the golf course to get a few swings in. I know those vultures will be out tomorrow at the course. I usually go to Shamrock golf course to work on chipping and driving the ball. I don't hit many balls. I think it gets boring after so many. Shamrock is a golf course run by a group of old golfers that all chipped in to keep it going when the economy got bad. I get me a small bucket and try to hit the flags and free my mind up a little.

Locked Up they want let me out,
No they want let me out.
Maybe a visit they want let me out

Send me some magazines they won't let me out

Send me some money orders

Me: Hello

Charita: you know Amari has practice today.

Me: O yeah, I forgot, I'll be there in a minute.

Amari keeps a busy schedule. She is a high jumper with the Durham Striders, a track club out of Durham. They are a serious group of coaches and athletes. I volunteer as the high jump coach and help out where I can. 40 minutes later, we were out at Cummings High School track, watching the kids go through their warm ups and, stretches. The kids have a good chance to get scholarships when they stick with the program. Coach Davis has produced some of the best athletes in North

Carolina. Coach has a way with the kids that is strict and cunning, especially with the premier athletes. Somehow, he can tell the kids what they couldn't do and they would rise to meet the challenge. This skill has won him 22 State Championships in track and field. Amari and the other high jumpers worked on pop ups, jumps, and back bends for our time and then we head home.

I love the drive home; it is relaxing and scenic with very few lights. Being home is always a highlight of the day. Charita was home when I walk in and I can smell the fried chicken, green beans and mashed potatoes and gravy. I don't do left overs often and chicken two times in one day is a no-no for me. I usually would have called home to see if

Charita had cooked anything and what she had.

Locked Up, they want let me out,
No... they want let me out.
Maybe a visit, they want let me out
Send me some magazines, they won't let me out
Send me some money orders

Me: hello

Operator: You have a call from an inmate at the Alamance County jail, Roberto Ruiz

Roberto Ruiz: Hey Doc, can you come and take me out of jail?

Me: What are you in for?

Roberto: They got me here for DWI, but I was not driving the car when they came. I was in the liquor store.

Me: That don't sound right, you were in the liquor store? How much is your bond?

Roberto: I know right, the bond is twenty five hundred dollars; I got the money to bail out.

Me: Hey, are you any kin to Jesse Ruiz?

Roberto: Yeah that's my uncle Jesse.

Me: Ok, get in touch with Jesse, if he says he'll sign for you, I'll send Deva down to bail you out.

Roberto: Ok, thank you, thank you. (click)

In jail,
In jail without no bail,
In jail,
We're in jail, because we failed

Deva: Yeah

Me: Hey D, can you go get a Roberto Ruiz out of jail, he says he has the money down there.

Deva: Who's going to sign for him?

Me: His uncle Jesse, I know him from when I worked for the City, it shouldn't be a problem. O yeah, I'm going to play golf in the morning.

Deva: Ok I'll be at the office to open up. (click)

Early in the morning, I go down stairs and pray over my day. Thank you Lord for allowing me to see another day, then I pray for my wife and kids. Next, I go to the Weider 9655 Universal machine. it's an oldie but goodie. I've had it for over ten years. It is a complete work out with bench press, leg extinctions, military press, and squats. I do two out of the four each day. After two sets of thirty, I move to the Elliptical Machine for twenty minutes, all while watching ESPN and local news. After a quick shave and shower, I'm out the door on my way to the golf course. Today we are playing Indian Valley, the City's public course. None of the guys I play with have a private course membership, we play so many different courses in a year it just wouldn't make sense, plus they would rather bet it on the course. The Valley is my favorite course, since they have a Memorial to my Mom on hole number eighteen. She loved to play with her coworkers from the Hospital. She worked in the Emergency room for thirty-two years on the night shift. I think the night shift ladies got to be close because of all the drama coming in.

Locked Up, they want let me out,

No... they want let me out.

Maybe a visit, they want let me out

Send me some magazines they want let me out

Send me some money orders

Me: Hello

Deva: Hey Doc, you remember yesterday, when I told you we had two forfeitures come in yesterday.

Me: (Staying quiet for 15 secs.) yeah.

Deva: Hope I didn't mess him up on that shot. Well, the other guy, Bobby Tucker, I hear he is over in Marrytown.

Me: Ok, where at?

(other golfers in the background talking: I got a 5, I got 4)

Deva: He's staying with Sophia over off Fifth Street, what time will you be done?

Me: I should be done by 3:30. I'll give you a call when I'm heading that way.

Deva: Cool.

After I finished paying the vultures, I call Deva and meet him at the Office. We load up for the hunt for Bobby. The Marrytown community has a lot going on; a couple of competing liquor houses, several drug houses and some prostitutes sprinkled in. I drive the Avalon this time, since it is still daytime.

Deva gives a call to our informant, who said Bobby had been going back and forth to the Quickie Mart all day. They also said that he had gotten into a fight a couple of days ago and cut somebody. Bobby is around 52 years old and well known by both Deva and myself. He is about six foot two and lean for a man around his age. He wears a mustache and has a small scar on the side of his face from some old prison fight back in the day. We turn down Morehead and see a guy fitting Bobby's description walking in the same direction with his back to us. We keep cruising until he really comes into focus, so that we can make a positive identification.

He looked like he didn't have a care in the world, from his casual stride. The alcohol he's been consuming all day probably helped. I pull up on Deva's side of the car and Deva jumps out right in front of him. His eyes get big and he takes off around the back of my car and across the street. I slam the car in park and jump out yelling.

Me: Are you seriously trying to run, you know we are way too old for this!

Bobby makes it half way across the yard on the other side of the street, when I corner him off. He throws his hands up like he wanted to fight, but while he was focusing on me. Deva comes in from the side, picks him up and slams him to the ground with all three hundred and forty pounds on top of him. I hear the air come out of him. He reaches for his pocket; I grab his wrist and twisted it toward his back.

Bobby: Ok, Ok you got me, let up on my arm man, I think I pulled something in my leg.

Me: Man you know we are too old for this, fifty three year olds need to stretch twenty minutes to run one minute.

Bobby: I'm fifty-two, Doc. I was going to turn myself in.

Me: Where at, behind the house? Help him up, Deva.

I hook Bobby up behind his back with the lucky Smith and Wesson handcuffs, then give Bobby a quick once over. We pull his box cutter out of his front pocket. Bobby gets placed in the front seat beside me and big Deva squeezes into the back. The conversation on the way to the jail is light and

Bobby is somewhat apologetic. We have been getting him out for so long and now, I think, he knows our working relationship was over. I pulled up to the security gate at the jail and pushed the buzzer.

(Buzz...)
Jail Staff: Yes, can I help you.
Me: This is Doc, I'm bringing one in.
Jail Staff: Alright Doc

(Buzz...)
The gate started to slowly open and I pull down to the sally port and waited for it to open, soon the sally port garage door opened, on the right side. I pulled up as far as I could. There are a couple of police cars parked ahead

of me. One is from Burlington City Police and the other from Elon City Police. We put our guns and tasers in the trunk and pull Bobby out.

Bobby: I lost my reading glasses when Deva tackled me in the grass.

Me: Call your girl and see if she can go over there and look for them. What do you want me to do with your box cutter?

Bobby: Keep it. I don't need it in here.

I chuck the box cutter in the front seat and lock the doors. Usually, I just drop Deva at the gate and he'll walk them in so I can go on, but today I go in through the double security doors to the jail. Deva had told me that the procedures had been changed and I want to check them out. That metal on metal sound lets you know there's no escaping. The officers have two people in custody ahead of us to see the Magistrate.

Arrestee: Hey Doc, I was getting ready to call you.
Me: O yeah, what's going on?
Arrestee: Man, they got me hear on some bogus charges they pulled me and I was in my yard. I was home. How could I get a DWI in my yard?
Me: Call your people and tell them to give me a call.

The officer with the arrestee gives me a little smile to say, "you know he's lying, right"? I give him a big grin back, which implies I understand the message. Deva and I get our surrender sheet and leave. We are going to have to file it with the courts the next day since court closed at five. It is close to 6:30 in the evening, I drop Deva off at his SUV. Deva drives a Cadillac Escalade with twenty-inch rims and a boom box in the back.

Locked Up, they want let me out,
No... they want let me out.
Maybe a visit, they want let me out
Send me some magazines, they want let me out
Send me some money orders

Me: Reaves

Carter: Hey Doc, I need to see how to set this phone up, I got my daughters old phone and I can't work my ring tones.

Me: Ok, what kind of phone is it?

Carter: It's a Samsung. I'll bring it down there in the morning sometime. what time are you going to be in?

Me: I'll be there by ten at least, if not Latina will be there, she can show you how to set it up.

Carter: I'd rather she showed me anyway.

Me: What are you saying?

Carter: She's better at explaining and a whole lot cuter.

Carter's married to a beautiful, active woman named Mary. She bowls, plays tennis and walks every morning. She really lights up a room when she shows up, I'm sure that rubs off on Carter. He's always laughing and smiling. Don't be fooled, he is a powerful tough old codger. He comes by and tells me stories about when he was in the Military or when he played football at Winston Salem State University. Carter also has a real powerful deep voice. Barry White would be jealous of his laugh; it vibrates the room. I decide to shut it down for day and head home.

Phone ringing.

Charita: hello

Me: Hey, what are you eating tonight.

Charita: Well, I didn't do any cooking today, me and Amari's eating sandwiches.

Me: I'll grab something then.

Charita: These sandwiches are tasty, I got some Rubens.

Me: That's Ok, see you soon.

Charita knows I don't like sauerkraut, so it must not have been a good day at the school. Sometimes she'll take a substitute job at the elementary school. The kids like to give the subs a hard time. She really has a good temperament for it and uses simple methods. She will send the troublemakers to the office or use her whistle, but if all else fails, she pushes the emergency button. The principle will come down and stare at the kids until they get nervous. Charita has a great personality and sense of humor. Being from a family with six siblings, she knows how to hold her own in a dozen's contest. She also likes to save money and sometimes that can be a little embarrassing, especially, when she is across the store telling me to put something back because she saw a cheaper Food Lion brand. She is constantly trying to get me to get the off brand of everything.

The next morning, I take Amari to school so that Charita can go back to South Graham Elementary for a second round with the kids. We pull up on the school with the principle outside directing the traffic, one line from the same direction, no cutting in from the left, which stops traffic both ways, it saves everybody time.

Me: You know you have practice this evening.
Amari: I know, who's coming to pick me up.
Me: Your Mom will be here this evening. Do your best.
Amari: I will.

When I get to the office Latina was there already.

Latina: Did you know Jerry Jones, the guy with Calvin Lang was in jail in Orange County for murder? They said he and some guys robbed and killed a drug dealer named Whiz outside of a Hillsborough night club.

Me: Wow, I guarantee Calvin was with him.

Latina: Probably.

I hate it when I get someone out of jail and, they do something crazy. It really pisses me off when I don't follow my instincts, especially when someone gets hurt or killed. I saw that look on his face, I'll remember that look for a long time.

Me: Where did they pick him up?

Latina: He was at Sam's quickie mart on Highway 70. His girl friend called the police on him. She was scared of him after he came home jacked up on something talking about the killing.

Latina: Whiz was well liked and the witnesses also called the police.

Me: What did they say about the people with him?

Latina: Two other guys, but they had on masks.

In jail,
In jail without no bail,
In jail,
We're in jail, because we failed

Me: Hey Deva we need to ride tonight, I want to try and put Calvin's case to rest.

Deva: What time you want to meet up?

Me: Nine at the office.

Deva: I'll be there.

June walks into the office after I hang up with Deva and tells me to put "it" in the bucket. The office is a total glass front, with Reaves Real Estate Inc. on one side, and Reaves Bail Bonds on the other. Inside the glass window I have a chessboard with two chairs on either side similar to a checkerboard set up in a barbershop. Golf equipment lines the north wall with two putting cups on opposite sides of the room.

The bucket is where we put our dollars for our putt off. We take three balls and putt to the cup, the one with the most makes, gets the dollar. After I lose a total of three dollars for the day, I get on the phone with some of my informants about Calvin and Alex. No one really knows where Calvin is; however, they did know what he liked to do. Calvin liked to drink liquor out of small liquor bottles.

Earlier, when Latina went to the mailbox, she brought back a small empty liquor bottle. I think it is a message from Calvin to let me know he had been by. My urgency to find him rises to a maximum level. I had put out a one hundred dollar reward for Calvin and Alex. I know it won't be too long before someone will call. Most people were scared to death of Calvin. Alex is a different story. He isn't a bad guy. He is just a hustler that sold drugs with no violence in his history.

At nine, Deva pulls up. I give Deva an update on Jerry and about finding the liquor bottle in my mailbox.

Deva: That would be a little bold don't you think?

Me: I know, but who else would have done it. I got a list of places he goes in Burlington.

Deva: He can't stay here, we know way too many people for that.

The whole night we search from one hood to the other. We talk and show pictures. Everybody that knows him, know of someone he had shot. We decide to talk to one of the shooting victims. We chose Roberto since his name had come up and we had recently got him out of jail. When we get to Roberto's house, he tells us to come on in, he doesn't want to talk outside in front of the neighbors.

Roberto has a mobile home, in Green Level trailer park. He is a heavy set Mexican with a strong accent.

Me: Have you seen Calvin lately.

Roberto: Who?

Me: C Murk.

Roberto: Hey man, you and everyone else is looking for that fool! If I see him, you may be out of luck.

Me: What happened with you and him.

Roberto: I used to deal with him and Jerry all the time. One day, Jerry calls me and wanted to come by with some new product he had. When he got here, Jerry is looking crazy, so I ask him, "he got a problem"? He pulled out a gun and says I shorted him last time. C Murk came in from outside and tied me up in a chair. He had on a black mask, but I know it was him. Who else could it be? Jerry point the gun at my head, I knew I was dead. Click, it don't fire. Then he laugh and say, "this your lucky day", where is the money. I gave them my cash and stash. He told me if I say anything, he would be back. I thought it was over, but on the way out the door C Murk looks back and shoots me in the leg.

Me: Wow, you should be retired after that one.

Roberto: Bro, I pissed myself, but I have people, he messed with the wrong guy.

Since no one has seen Calvin in Alamance County lately, Deva and I head over to Calvin's girlfriends apartment. Deva and I mostly talk about sports while we are on our hunt.

Deva: I think college athletes should get paid.
Me: Why, they get a lot of perks clothes, free education, food and sometimes they even get shopping money.
Deva: That's true, but I know what it's like when the cafeteria closes and you don't have any money to get something to eat, that's ruff.

While riding out with Deva on a hunt sometimes a little trepidation will seep in about my car seats. Deva leans way back in the car seat. I think back to when Deva was in college and he was driving a little Subaru and his driver side car seat broke. The way his driver seats would lean on the right side from the pressure he applied over time. Deva is a big powerful man, no two ways about it. I don't think he realizes his own strength.

Fifteen minutes later we pull into the apartment complex, it was about eleven thirty at night and all her lights are off. We cruise past her car slow, and then stop a few cars down. I get out and feel her hood. It was cold. I don't see a lot going on. We take a quick walk around the apartment, hoping to hear someone talking inside or see someone moving around. We go back to the car and decided to go to another well known apartment complex to try and find someone who knows Calvin or get lucky and see him.

When we get there, the first thing I notice is there are a lot of moving around for the middle of the night. It looked like a zombie movie. People were being drawn to the drugs like a beacon. My car doesn't get noticed as much in Hillsborough as it does in Burlington. We ride through unnoticed until I get behind the apartments. I spot two guys running from the side of the apartments, full speed, coming at us. Both guys have their hands in their pockets, as if they were pulling something out. I pull first and aim the barrel of my Glock forty right at the guy on the left's chest. They are about seven feet away when they both slide and fall backward. Drugs drop to the ground and their hands fly up. I feel something touching my right shoulder and glanced to see Deva holding his Glock directly beside my face aimed at the young men. They look like teenagers around fifteen years old, I tell them to get up and get gone. They tear off running like their lives depend on it. I get out of the car and crush the crack in the little plastic baggies. We drive off.

Me: What were you doing D?
Deva: I was going with you, you pull, I pull.
Me: I think we've been going at it a little hard, let's head in and take a couple of days off to decompress
Deva: Sounds good to me, they have a wrestling Smack Down coming on this

weekend, I'm getting it on pay per view, if you want to swing through.

Me: Thanks Deva, I appreciate the offer.

Deva was just pulling my chain on coming over, he knows I wouldn't even watch female nude wrestling. The phone rang all night long, "Locked up they want let me out", "I'm Locked up" Even on the days we chill, the phone never stops. I get the 3:00 a.m. DWI calls, the late night domestic fight calls, it seems like someone's always going to jail. Saturday Morning, I get up and get ready for a good golf round. Everybody tries to come out on the weekends and show what they've got. Most of the time, it's a lot of the regulars, but sometimes we have some outside hustlers come and try to take our skin money. Skins are a portion of a ten dollar "ante". The "ante" is a pool of money collected from each golfer. The money is divided by hole and is called a "skin". Whoever shoots the low score on a hole gets a "skin". The weather really cooperates and for some reason and with little to no sleep, I beat June and he had to hand over three bucks.

Me: I believe I will have a June Deluxe meal today.

June: It better not cost more than a Happy meal or you're going to be short of money.

Me: Thanks for the suggestion, Hey, June where are you going to watch the Super Bowl Sunday.

June: I'm going to watch it at home, I'm Sixty Seven years old, I get sleepy by the second half, if it ain't no good.

The thought hits me at that moment, no one's expecting uninvited visitors on Super Bowl Sunday.

In jail,
In jail without no bail,
In jail,
We're in jail, because we failed

Deva: Sup

Me: How was the Smack Down?

Deva: It was Great, The Rock showed up.

Me: Hey, lets go down and try Calvin on Sunday before the Super Bowl starts.

Deva: Cool, I'll meet you at the office around four.

When we get to Christie's apartment, everything is quiet and calm. The temperature was about fifty degrees. We parked right in front of the apartment. Deva pulls out the pistol grip pump shotgun from my trunk and posts up near the side of the house. I approach and knock on the front door. I knock again with more force this time. I can hear the TV playing preludes to the Super Bowl. I call out, "Hey, Christie, it's Doc Reaves", "Bail Bondsman". I hear a bump from inside and then I hear the little voice of her four year old say, "Momma said she can't come to the door right now". I pull back from the door and call 911.

911 Operator: 911 Operator what is your emergency.

Me: I am Michael Doc Reaves, I'm a Bail Bondsman from Alamance County I have a subject in the Vine apartments and I need an officer to stand by while I make entry.

911: Do you have a warrant.

Me: I have a Forfeiture requesting his arrest.

911: We're busy, but I'll get a car coming when they clear.

Deva waits by the car with a straight line view into the apartment hallway and I go to the corner of the apartment with an angle to watch each window. After about fifteen minutes, a patrol car pulls up with two officers inside. They get out looking like they were coming from lunch. Both officers are slim and look like they have been on the force two or three years.

Officer 1: Ok, you call about a skip in the apartment?

Me: Yes, sir.

Officer 1: Who's in there?

Me: Calvin Lang

Both officers pull guns. They look like Barney Fife from the Andy Griffith Show, wide-eyed and nervous.

Officer 2: Do-you-know-anything-about-Calvin Lang!

Me: They say he's a dangerous guy.

Both officers look at each other as though this was their last day on the job, and said "ok". Their first step is toward the door of the apartment. I had holstered my weapon when the officers pulled up. I pull it back out and follow them to the door. Deva goes to the corner of the apartment. The Officers and I approached the front door. I spoke firmly, "Reaves Bail Bonds". "I need you to open the door". Ten seconds go by and then 30 more seconds. I yell again, "Reaves Bail Bonds"! "Open the door" or "I'm going to kick it in". The door opens and Calvin Lang sticks his hands out in front of him. Officers 1 said, "we'll take him" and place him in handcuffs.

They told us to meet them at the office. While in the office, the officers were trying to find the detective that had taken out the warrants for him almost two years ago. They never find the detective. Anyway, the warrants they have are so old that they are out of date. Plus, with the Super Bowl on, the officer couldn't get anyone to answer their phones. Officer 1 told us that we should take him to Alamance County, since they would give him a bigger bond, than they would in Orange. I hooked him up with my lucky Smith and Wesson's and loaded him in the Avalon. On the way to the jail, Calvin is pissed, but decides to ask.

Calvin: What's on that warrant anyway.

Me: It's for shooting the Club owner in Hillsborough.

Calvin: O, he ain't going to talk I already talked to him.

Me: O yeah...

Calvin: I'm not going to be there long.

Me: Don't matter to me, long as I get my surrender sheet. I'm good, what I want to know is, "did you put those liquor bottles in my mailbox"?

Calvin: Come on man, you know I don't play no games like that.

Me: I can't believe you came out of the house like you did.

Calvin: I'm not going to start shooting with my son in there.

When we get to the jail with Calvin, the Magistrate gave him a Ten thousand dollar bond and put a hold on him for the SBI. We get our papers and I drive Deva around to the office and his car. I head home for the second half of the game.

Locked Up, they want let me out,
No… they want let me out.
Maybe a visit, they want let me out
Send me some magazines, they won't let me out
Send me some money orders

Me: Reaves…

Poochie: Hey Doc, are you still looking for Alex?